Andrew Matthews was born in Barry in Wales. He studied History and English at Reading University before training to be a teacher. After he graduated, he took up a teaching post at Yateley Comprehensive School, where he taught English for many years, frequently using his pupils as the inspiration for his writing. Now a full-time writer, Andrew has published over thirty books including *Monsoon Taggert's Amazing Finishing Academy* (Methuen), which was nominated for the Smarties Award, and *Cat Song* (Hutchinson), which was nominated for the Mother Goose Award and shortlisted for the Smarties Award. Many of his books have also been recorded as audio books by such distinguished actors as Jennifer Saunders, Brian Glover and Willy Rushden. Andrew currently lives in Reading with his wife and cats.

Christian Birmingham was brought up in Surrey and Cornwall. After sixth form college, he went to Exeter College of Art and Design where he graduated in illustration. His first book was *The Night Before Christmas* (Running Press), which was closely followed by *Dancing Bear*, written by Michael Morpugo, and an illustrated edition of Charles Dicken's *Oliver Twist* (both HarperCollins). In addition Christian has worked for several design groups, completing two sets of Royal Mail stamps to celebrate the centenaries of Enid Blyton and Rugby League. Christian is currently living in London.

To Doris and Guthrie ❖ A.M

First published in Great Britain in 1995 by
Frances Lincoln Limited, 4 Torriano Mews,
Torriano Avenue, London NW5 2RZ

First paperback edition 2000

British Library Cataloguing in Publication Data available on request

ISBN 0-7112-0980-4 hardback
ISBN 0-7112-1357-7 paperback

Set in Berkeley
Printed in Hong Kong

1 3 5 7 9 8 6 4 2

TOD
and the
Clock
Angel

Andrew Matthews

Illustrated by

Christian Birmingham

FRANCES LINCOLN

Tod had nothing; he had no one. He lived alone in the forest. He drank from streams and pools and ate what he could find. When he couldn't find food, he went to the village on the edge of the forest at night. He watched through the branches of the trees, and waited until the people were asleep. Then he crept into the village to take food from their cottages. Tod never asked, he always stole.

The villagers did not know who took the food. They thought the village was haunted.

One winter, cold came into the forest like a white wolf. It went looking for Tod. Tod woke up at sunrise and saw frost furring the bare branches. Mist hung in the air like wolf-breath. The cold reached through Tod's rags and touched his skin with its sharp claws.

"I must run," said Tod, "or the cold will sink its ice teeth in my heart." He ran to the village to find shelter, but the villagers heard him coming.

"It's the ghost! The ghost is walking!" they cried.

They locked their doors and barred their windows and set loose their fiercest dogs to chase Tod away. They were too frightened to look and see that he was no ghost.

Tod ran from the dogs. He went to places in the forest he had never been before, but the cold found him. It pressed its paws on the streams and froze them. It made the earth hard.

"If I don't find shelter soon, this cold will freeze me stiffer than stone," said Tod.

He ran until he came to a high wall that blocked his way. He climbed the wall, and on the other side he saw a great house, with dark and broken windows.

"I could hide in there," said Tod. "The dogs and the cold will never find me!"

Silent as a shadow, Tod jumped down from the wall and went to the back of the house. He found a stone staircase that led down to an old door. The door was half-open, and Tod slipped inside.

He was in a cellar, where things had been put away and forgotten. Moonlight came in thinly through a dingy window. Cobwebs shook in the draught from the door and the air smelled of mould.

A dim shape caught Tod's eye. It was a tall clock, and as he stared at it, it stared back at him with its white face. There were suns and moons painted on the clock's dial, and on its dusty case was a sad-faced angel with wings like a swan's.

Tod went closer and trod on something hard. It was a key, decorated with suns and moons. Tod saw a small hole under the hands of the clock. He reached up and opened the door that covered the clock's dial, fitted the key into place and turned it.

The clock made a skittering noise, like the nails of rats scampering over slate. It made a pattering noise, like rain falling into deep dust. It ticked; and tocked; and talked. Its voice was brass cogs, and coiled iron, and time going round in circles.

"Tod!" it said. "Let in the moon."

Tod was not afraid. He climbed a sagging stack of boxes, yanked a rusty catch and creaked the cellar window open. The moonlight beamed in and made the clock shine.

"Now!" sighed the clock, and with its springs and levers it span the moonlight into wings, with feathers as pale and soft as snowflakes. With its weights and wheels, it span itself into an angel, who looked at Tod and held out his hand.

"I am Taruminel," the angel said. "I have waited a long time for you to come and set me free."

"Me?" said Tod.

"You," Taruminel said. He looked at Tod and Tod saw that his eyes were sad and kind. "It's time for your story to begin, tonight of all nights. Do you know what night this is?"

"A hungry night," said Tod, "and cold, and dark as death."

"This night is Christmas Eve," smiled Taruminel, "the Night of Angels. Take my hand."

Tod touched the clock angel's fingers. A sparking and
crackling ran through his blood and made him warm.
    "What's that feeling?" he cried.
    "Safety," said Taruminel. "It's what stays inside you when
your loneliness has gone away. Come!"

Taruminel spread his wings and lifted Tod up. Out through the window they flew, rising into the night sky. When they were higher than mountains, Taruminel stopped and hovered, scooping the air with his wings.

"Look up, Tod," he said.

Tod saw the moon, round as a clock-face. He saw the swirling stars, as tiny and bright as specks of dust turning in sunlight.

"Now watch," said Taruminel, "and listen."

Taruminel sang in a voice as deep as a bell tolling the last chime of midnight. It made the sky shiver and ripple like the surface of a pool. In the distance an angel appeared, falling out of the night as fast as a falling star; then another, and another until angels were dropping on to the sleeping earth in a dazzling rain.

The angels sang. Their voices joined in with Taruminel's until it seemed that all the bells in the world were ringing at once.

The song of the angels got inside Tod. He danced in the air, and the stars and the moon waltzed over his head.

"Why am I dancing?" he laughed.

"Because you're happy," Taruminel told him.

"Happy," said Tod. "I like it better than cold and hungry."

"Hold my hand tightly," said Taruminel.
He shut his wings and they dropped out of the sky.
The wind hissed and zipped through the clock angel's feathers.
It whistled loudly in Tod's ears and fluttered his hair around
his head.

The dark earth rushed up to meet them, but just as it was
about to smash them, Taruminel swooped. Tod's insides
seemed to turn round in a circle that made him close his
eyes. When he opened them, he found that Taruminel was
flying low over a river.

They skimmed under bridges and over the top-masts of tall ships at anchor. They flew out to sea, where waves with silver crests rolled slowly beneath them. Icebergs as big as villages gleamed in the moonlight as Tod and Taruminel swept past.

They crossed over snowy peaks and silent deserts and a great city, whose lights glittered like a web of jewels.

"I never knew the world was so wide!" gasped Tod.

"On this night, of all nights, you came to the house and set me free from my curse," said Taruminel. "Now it's time for me to free you. Tonight is the Night of Angels, and the Night of Children, and it's time to begin again."

They fell towards the earth as gently as mist curling, and
landed outside a village. Tod saw candle-flames flickering
like waving fingers in the windows of the cottages. There were
branches of holly on the doors. Tod could hear voices singing
and children laughing.

   "This is the village I ran away from!" said Tod. "I can't
begin here! They think I'm a ghost!"

   "You must," said Taruminel. "Just knock on any door.
Now you can tell them about safety and happiness and
the wide world. They won't turn you away."

Right in front of Tod stood a cottage whose candle-flames
seemed to beckon. He let go of Taruminel's hand, took a few
steps forward, then felt afraid and looked back over his shoulder.
There was nothing there but the darkness of the forest,
where the white wolf lay in wait. He took all his courage,
walked up to the cottage door, and knocked.

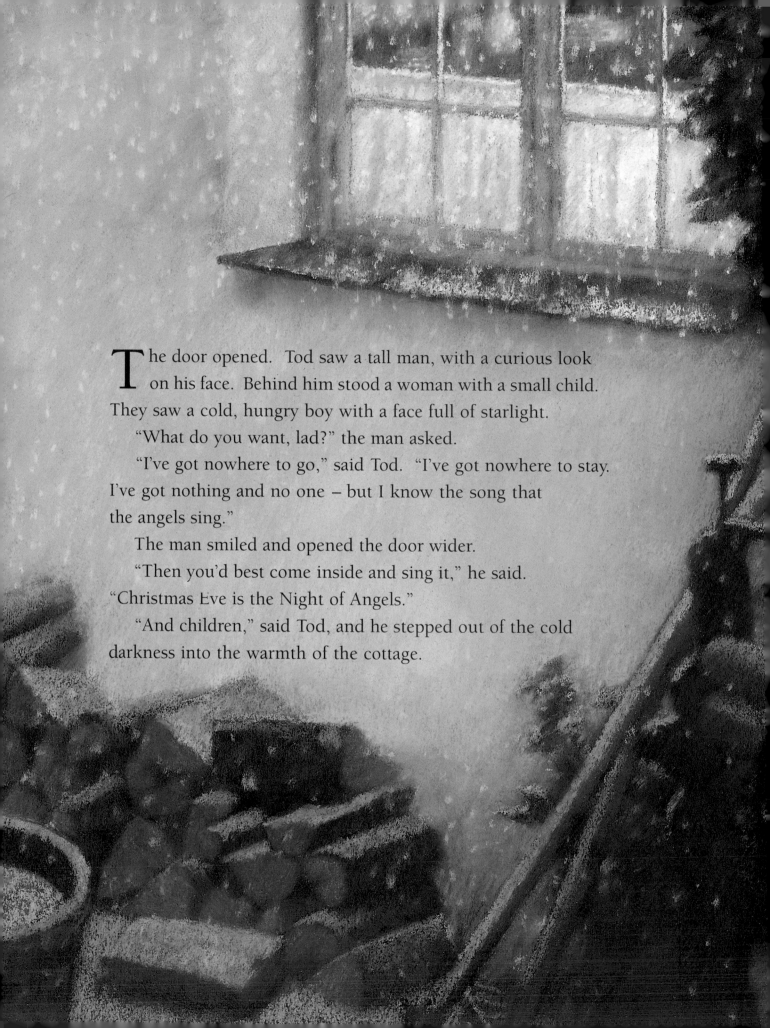

The door opened. Tod saw a tall man, with a curious look on his face. Behind him stood a woman with a small child. They saw a cold, hungry boy with a face full of starlight.

"What do you want, lad?" the man asked.

"I've got nowhere to go," said Tod. "I've got nowhere to stay. I've got nothing and no one – but I know the song that the angels sing."

The man smiled and opened the door wider.

"Then you'd best come inside and sing it," he said. "Christmas Eve is the Night of Angels."

"And children," said Tod, and he stepped out of the cold darkness into the warmth of the cottage.

MORE PICTURE BOOKS IN PAPERBACK FROM FRANCES LINCOLN

A PUSSYCAT'S CHRISTMAS
Anne Mortimer

Here is Christmas seen from a cat's-eye view, as one little pussycat finds feathery snow to pounce on, coloured paper to rip and tangerines and holly to sniff. A heart-warming celebration of Christmas decorated with exquisite water-colours.

Suitable for National Curriculum English – Reading, Key Stage 1
Scottish Guidelines English Language – Reading, Levels B and C

ISBN 0-7112-0970-0 £4.99

THE SNOWCHILD
Debi Gliori

Poor left-out Katie doesn't know how to play. She has lots of good ideas – but she's always out of step with the other children's games. Then, one winter's morning, Katie wakes up and decides to build a snowman...

Suitable for National Curriculum English – Reading, Key Stages 1 and 2
Scottish Guidelines English Language – Reading, Levels A and B

ISBN 0-7112-0894-8 £4.99

THE SNOW WHALE
Caroline Pitcher
Illustrated by Jackie Morris

One November morning, when the hills are hump-backed with snow, Laurie and Leo decide to build a snow whale. As they shovel, pat and polish it out of the hill, the whale gradually takes on a life of its own.

Suitable for National Curriculum English – Reading, Key Stage 1
Scottish Guidelines English Language – Reading, Levels A and B

ISBN 0-7112-1093-4 £4.99

Frances Lincoln titles are available from all good bookshops.
Prices are correct at time of publication, but may be subject to change.